THE MURDER OF HOUND DOG

I dug Hound Dog Bates's grave right smack in the middle of the yard, right where the porch-sitting aunts and everybody who came to call could see it. Right smack in the middle of Aunt Faith's pansy bed.

I dug and sweated and glared at buzzards, buzzards who'd like to eat my poisoned dog, and reckoned more tear water ran out of me than in all my other twelve years put together. When I got through burying Hound Dog Bates (and I buried him in my best shirt, too), I patted the dirt down hard and went to the barn for a hammer and nails. I made a cross and with my pocket knife I carved: "Here lies Hound Dog Bates who was made deader than a doornail with ground-up glass or somethin else cruel, murdered by aunt or aunts unknown. I, his master, will git even fer him. Signed, Sassafras Bates."

"A vivid setting and interesting protagonist. . . . There is appealing spirit here, and enough mystery to intrigue."
—*Booklist*

"The [book's] strengths . . . are the wonderful characters who face their hard life with determination and the strong portrayal of life on a poor dirt farm." —*School Library Journal*

THE MURDER OF HOUND DOG BATES

A NOVEL BY

ROBBIE BRANSCUM

PUFFIN BOOKS

PUFFIN BOOKS
Published by the Penguin Group
Penguin Books USA Inc., 375 Hudson Street, New York, New York 10014, U.S.A.
Penguin Books Ltd, 27 Wrights Lane, London W8 5TZ, England
Penguin Books Australia Ltd, Ringwood, Victoria, Australia
Penguin Books Canada Ltd, 10 Alcorn Avenue, Toronto, Ontario, Canada M4V 3B2
Penguin Books (N.Z.) Ltd, 182-190 Wairau Road, Auckland 10, New Zealand

Penguin Books Ltd, Registered Offices: Harmondsworth, Middlesex, England

First published in the United States of America by The Viking Press, 1982
Published in Puffin Books, 1995

1 3 5 7 9 10 8 6 4 2

THE LIBRARY OF CONGRESS HAS CATALOGED THE VIKING PRESS EDITION AS FOLLOWS:
Branscum, Robbie.
The murder of Hound Dog Bates.
Summary: When Sassafras Bates finds his dog dead,
he suspects that one of his three spinster aunts is the murderer.
[1. Mystery and detective stories. 2. Dogs—Fiction. 3. Aunts—Fiction.
4. Mountain life—Fiction. 5. Arkansas—Fiction.] I. Title.
PZ7.B73754Mu [Fic] 82-1911 ISBN 0-670-49521-2 AACR2

Puffin Books ISBN 0-14-037593-7

Printed in the United States of America

To Tom Hunniutt,
the man who makes songs and music

To Pat Gievet,
for being there

To Hugh Agee,
who is a great person, but thinks I am

To the beautiful Deborahs in my life

CHAPTER 1

The hot sun of an Arkansas summer beat down on my back and head. The hot dust of the ground burned my bare feet and hands. It beat down on the form I knelt over.

I raised my head to glare up at the red-orange sky, at the cloud of black buzzards circling around, getting lower and lower. Heat dried the tears on my face into a dirty crust, and I raised my fist to the buzzards, screaming, "Ye git! Ye git! Ye jest git, ye nasty rotten ol' birds!"

I looked madly around for something to dig with. I didn't dare leave Hound Dog Bates to get a shovel, for iffen I did, them buzzards would have him gone in a few gulps.

All I saw were rocks, big and little, 'cause the part of Arkansas where we lived was full of them. But I couldn't see a stick or anything sharp to dig with.

I looked up again. The buzzards were getting lower and lower, and suddenly I knew what I was going to do. I was going to bury Hound Dog Bates right under the nose of the murderer. Right where the mean killer could see the grave of the poor critter they had cold-bloodedly killed—every time they stepped out of the house.

Having decided, I felt better and unbuckled my overall straps so I could get my shirt off. I wrapped the body of my dog in the shirt and, picking him up, staggered down the narrow dirt road to the old leaning farmhouse. The buzzards followed me in the sky.

I'd never noticed how dry and bleak the world looked before, then I reckoned maybe it was because I was carrying the only thing I had ever loved, and it was dead. I figured maybe I'd died too, died when I'd seen my dog lying stiff as Aunt Hope's starched drawers, stiff sorta jumping on the clothesline 'cause they weren't limp enough to flop in the breeze.

I figured maybe I'd gone to hell also. I mean, it didn't seem reasonable that it could get this hot on earth. Aunt Faith said aggravating things were sent to try us, and I for one was darned tired of being tried. 'Sides, she never said who was doing it—sending the aggravations, I mean. 'Sides, I figured it was somebody right here on this earth who'd killed my dog, and it wasn't no aggravation, just plain mean murder.

Sweat itched me between my shoulder blades, but I couldn't lay my dog down to scratch. The buzzards might try to snatch a bite of him. Sweat dripped in my eyes, stinging, and the sun kept beating down. Even the hills had lost the greenness of spring many weeks ago, and the trees hung limp and thirsty-looking. The heat of the summer had sucked the color from the wild flowers, and the dry breeze rustled the long brown grass, making a noise like an old tired rattlesnake.

Even the farmhouse I could see in the distance seemed to lean farther with age. The silver of the wood had turned a dirty gray, and the picket fence looked like a giant's snaggle-toothed grin, there were so many broken pickets.

I couldn't remember no other place, for I was born in that house, and I reckoned I'd die in it— no doubt murdered like Hound Dog Bates, I told myself darkly.

I could see the inside of the house in my mind as well as if I'd been in it. There were four rooms: two bedrooms, a living room, a kitchen. All the furniture had been made by my grandpa and his grandpa long before I was born.

I stopped to rest, looking up to see how close the buzzards were before I lay my dog down to wipe sweat from my face. They had flown to high dots in the burning sky. I sat down beside the dog's body and felt tears come close again. That dog was all I'd ever had of my very own, and in my head I could see pictures of him as a puppy— white with black spots, ears so long they nigh touched the ground. I could feel his wiggly warm body when he slept with me winters or when we camped in the woods. And I remembered giving him my name 'cause it was all I had to give.

Hound Dog Bates didn't know he was a dog,

and it wasn't his fault. I mean, I never treated him like a dog. I mean, Aunt Hope ought to have known he only stole food because he couldn't understand why he had to eat on the floor when the rest of us sat at the table. After all, he slept like a human with his head on the pillow next to mine. 'Course he didn't know he wasn't supposed to. I just let him and never told.

When we went possum hunting on cold frosty nights, Hound Dog Bates slept right under the covers with me next to the campfire. We watched the stars pop out nigh close enough to touch, and the big cold fall moon ride the sky. Many a night I held his shaking body close and whispered in his ear 'cause he was dead afraid of the woods and dark and night things. I never told nobody he was a yellow coward, and I reckoned he was grateful. And I didn't never tell about him messing on himself when a strange, huge black dog raided our camp and stole our supper, 'cause truth to tell I nigh messed my own self and could have swore the dog was a bear. I reckon Hound Dog Bates died thinking he was nigh ate by a bear once.

Now tears came, for now I didn't have nobody

of my own, nobody atall, 'cause Ma had died birthing me and Pa had drifted off a few weeks later, leaving me with Ma's sisters, my aunts, to raise me. There were three of them, old-maid women with sharp noses, harsh voices, dried-up bodies, more full of vinegar than piss, I reckoned. And one of them was a murderer.

None of them had ever liked Hound Dog Bates, even when he was a puppy. They took the broom to him if he ever even looked like he was thinking of peeing in the house, for all the aunts were nasty-nice clean. Why, they wouldn't have let me have a dog atall if Grandpa hadn't given him to me before he died.

I picked Hound Dog Bates up and staggered on under the hot sun. The heat of the dirt squashing up between my toes made me sorta hop on one foot, then the other. And I thought on the aunts, knowing it would be the hardest thing I ever done. I mean, trying to figure out who killed my dog, for the aunts were ever sneaky.

Aunt Hope, the youngest, thirty if she was a day, was goody-goody sneaky. I mean, she'd smile sweetly and take the last piece of cake or chicken. Though a body knowed she was a green-eyed greedy gut, running around eating the world up, a body couldn't say nothing, for her sweet-acting ways would make you look bad for saying anything atall.

She'd never liked Hound Dog Bates 'cause once when he was a puppy I grabbed the last piece of chicken and gave it to him, and since then Aunt Hope had watched us both with eagle eyes whenever there was food around.

Though Aunt Hope's nose was sharp, she was fatter than the other aunts. Fact of the matter, the bean poles in the garden were fatter than the other aunts. Aunt Hope had yellow hair and blue eyes. She messed around the house, cooking, canning, and cleaning. She sewed things, too.

Aunt Faith messed around outside, raising a big garden and chickens. She raised pigs and ducks and took care of the cow, and a body would think she'd love all animals, but it ain't so, 'cause she hated Hound Dog Bates. She said she had no use for any animal that couldn't be ate or worked. And she said Hound Dog Bates was a dead drag on three poor women trying to scratch a living out of rocks and hard dirt.

Aunt Faith was tall, with coal-black hair, colder

black eyes, and lips so thin they nigh disappeared. Her skin was the color of maple wood 'cause she was ever in the sun and weather.

Of all the aunts, I reckon I feared Aunt Veela the most. Maybe 'cause she was taller, meaner-looking, with small darty eyes the color of blue winter ice, and she was older too, nigh fifty, I reckon, 'cause Aunt Faith was close to forty.

Aunt Veela did the hard farming in the family. I mean, she plowed the fields, chopped down trees, and done what no other woman in our hills did. She wore the overalls Grandpa had left behind when he died. And she wore his old straw hat, and she smoked a corncob pipe. And she cussed. She cussed ol' Sauce, our mule, and whatever else that made her mad, and she'd cussed Hound Dog Bates every day of what she called his worthless life.

Aunt Veela walked in long strides, her red hair always flying from under her hat, her pipe clenched in her teeth, and folks stayed out of her way. Womenfolks, especially church-going womenfolks, didn't have nothing to do with us. Leastways no more than they could help. And Aunt Veela said we sure the hell wouldn't butt in where we wasn't wanted. I knowed that wasn't the dad-blamed truth 'cause Aunt Veela butted in wherever she pleased, and folks didn't talk back to her no more than her sisters and me did.

Staggering, sweating, and looking up at the buzzards that had circled lower, so low they made black shadows on the ground, I made it to the gate. I laid Hound Dog Bates on the ground and rested, peering around. Nobody was in sight, and I knowed they wouldn't be 'cause Aunt Veela was laying the corn behind the north forty, Aunt Faith would be in the garden, and Aunt Hope would be sewing on the old treadle sewing machine on the screened-in back porch, where I slept.

I eased around the house and got the shovel leaning on the storm cellar. I dashed back around and started digging Hound Dog Bates's grave right smack in the middle of the yard, right where the porch-sitting aunts and everybody who came to call could see it. Right smack in the middle of Aunt Faith's pansy bed.

I dug and sweated and glared at buzzards, buzzards who'd like to eat my poisoned dog, and reckoned more tear water ran out of me than in all my other twelve years put together. When I got through burying Hound Dog Bates (and I buried him in my best shirt, too), I patted the dirt down hard and went to the barn for a hammer and nails. I made a cross and with my pocket knife I carved: "Here lies Hound Dog Bates who was made deader than a doornail with ground-up glass or somethin else cruel, murdered by aunt or aunts unknown. I, his master, will git even fer him. Signed, Sassafras Bates."

CHAPTER 2

It took me a long time to carve Sassafras, and I
reckoned it was the dumbest name I'd ever heard
tell of for a boy. But Aunt Veela said they'd named
me that 'cause I was sassy-acting since the day I
was born. 'Course my name had been shortened
to just plain Sass long ago.

With the cross in place at the head of Hound
Dog Bates's grave and all the tears in me drained
out, I sat back on my heels. Looking up, I seen
the buzzards were just tiny dark specks in the sky,

looking for supper someplace else, I reckoned. Seemed everything inside me had drained away with the tears, and I felt tired clear to my bones. I didn't seem to have much feeling of any kind atall and didn't even fear Aunt Veela any more. 'Sides, all them aunts was just women, just old-maid women. And for the first time I could remember, a sorta hard proud feeling came up in me. I mean, I was a man, my own man. And I'd find out who killed Hound Dog Bates if it took the rest of my life, and when I did, they'd best watch out 'cause they was gonna be in big trouble. I didn't know yet just what I was going to do to them, but it was going to be 'most as bad as the ground glass Hound Dog Bates had ate.

Maybe I'd poison them with the black widow spiders that lived in the corner of the hayloft. Or maybe I'd get me ten dogs, all with bad kidneys and mean sharp teeth. If I had someplace to go, maybe I'd run away. But right now I was just too tired.

I got up and headed for the barn, carrying the spade. All my aunts had their work, and I had mine. Only my work was the kind that made women sorta sick, and in my mind I sneered at them. I mean, what was so bad about raking out barn stalls and chicken houses, for Pete's sake! I raked out the mule's and cow's stalls and put in fresh straw and grain for the night. I cleaned out the chicken house, raking all the manure into a pile to dry for fertilizer for the garden and corn. And all the time I worked, I felt the missing shadow of Hound Dog Bates, 'cause he'd followed me everywhere I went for nigh as long as I could remember.

I heard Aunt Veela come in from plowing and unharness ol' Sauce, and I could hear her and Aunt Faith talk as they milked the cow. I fed the hogs some bran and drew water from the well to wash up. The smell of the supper Aunt Hope was cooking came out the back door, and I could smell corn bread, frying potatoes, and the sharp tang of mustard greens.

The thought crossed my mind that maybe a poisoner once started might be hard to stop. I mean maybe they'd just get rid of anybody they didn't like. A tingle of fear shot through me. Maybe one of my aunts didn't like me no more. Maybe never had. Maybe all three of them hated my guts.

I went to the cellar for milk and butter and into the kitchen just ahead of Aunt Veela and Aunt Faith. The sun started down as we ate, bathing the kitchen in a red glow. It looked and felt like we were sitting in flames. The kitchen was boiling hot from the old black cast-iron cookstove. Sweat glistened on the aunts' faces, and I could feel it creeping down the backs of my legs and dripping off my chin.

I'll say one thing for the aunts—they were good eaters and never said nothing till the first plate of food was gulped down. As for me, I reckon it was the first meal in my life that I could remember when I wasn't hungry. I was missing Hound Dog Bates under the table at my feet. Peering closely at the aunts to see if there was guilt on any of their faces, I decided they were strangers to me. I mean, I really didn't know them at all, even though I had lived with them all my life.

Stranger still, none of them, not one, had asked me where Hound Dog Bates was. 'Course they never talked till after the first plate was ate up, but it looked to me like they'd leastways ask.

When Aunt Hope did speak, it wasn't about the dog. She helped herself to a second plate of beans and corn bread, the steam from the platter fogging up her glasses. Peering over the plate at me, she said, "Sass, whar is yer shirt? An' yore best one, I might remind ye."

"Buried it," I said, staring straight back at her.

"Buried it?" Aunt Hope and Aunt Faith said sharplike at the same time. "Why?"

"You'll see after supper," I said stubbornly. Before either could say anything else, Aunt Veela said, "Leave the boy be fer now."

So everyone went back to eating, all but me, and I went back to staring at the women, thinking again I really didn't know nothing about them atall. I mean, I knowed Grandpa'd left them the farm when he passed on. I wondered why they never married, 'cause all the womenfolks I knowed their age had long been wed and had younguns, and some Aunt Veela's age even had grand-younguns. On the other hand, maybe no man had married them 'cause the aunts were so mean and snappy. Though there were some yellow pictures taken when they were young that I'd seen, and truth to tell, the aunts looked sorta pretty in them.

Maybe men didn't marry them 'cause they hated dogs, I told myself darkly, for Arkansas was hound dog country and 'most every man I knowed had from one to a dozen dogs. Maybe if they had a man and the man mussed up the house, tracked in mud or something, they'd poison him. Just like Hound Dog Bates. Maybe they didn't have a man 'cause they were afraid he'd get the house dirty, I bet. That was why. And 'cause of men liking dogs.

Fact of the matter, maybe they'd had husbands and got rid of them before I was old enough to know it. Maybe Aunt Veela was covering up their bodies in the north forty she was always plowing. And maybe yer goin' plumb crazy, I thought to myself, pushing away from the table.

As always in summer weather, Aunt Veela said, "Leave the dishes till coolness, girls, and let's rest on the porch."

I could feel my heart start to thump, 'cause Aunt Veela might give me a skinning when she saw the grave smack in front of the porch, but it'd be worth it to me if I could find out who killed my dog.

I followed the aunts out on the porch, nigh bumping into Aunt Veela when she stopped to light her pipe. It was the last light before dark, and the cross on the grave showed up plain. The aunts didn't notice it at first. They sat down in their rockers, muttering and fretting like hens settling on a roost.

I sat on the porch with my feet hanging off the edge like I always did. Also, it was a good way to get a head start iffen I had to run.

It was Aunt Veela who seen it first. Sitting straight up in her chair, she peered out at the yard, saying, "What in the dad-gum tarnation is a cross doin' in our yard?"

"Cross? Cross?" the other aunts echoed, leaning forward in their rockers.

"Who put it thar?" Aunt Veela asked.

"Not me. Not me," the aunts echoed again.

"Ye know about that cross, Sass boy?" Aunt Veela said, pointing her corncob pipe at me.

"Know about it," I said, cold and harsh.

"What's it fer?" Aunt Hope asked.

"See fer yourself," I said, scaring myself with my boldness, yet thinking I'd never be meek to them women again.

Aunt Veela went first, followed by the other two. There was dead quiet while they read the carving on the wide flat boards of the cross. Then Aunt Hope and Aunt Faith swore they'd never in their

17

born days seen such sass in a youngun. But Aunt Veela took her long strides toward me, yanked me straight up till I was eye level with her, saying, "Now, boy, ye best explain some," and her voice tone meant no nonsense.

I stared back at her, mean as I could, saying, "I found Hound Dog Bates dead. He was killed by eatin' ground-up glass, an' I know ye all hated his guts, an' I know one of ye killed him deader than a doornail. An' I don't keer iffen ye skin me alive, I ain't gonna move him till one of ye confess t' his killin'."

"I didn't kill that dad-blamed dog, Sassafras Bates," Aunt Faith said nigh in my ear, making me jump, so Aunt Veela set me down none too gently.

"Why, we didn't even know he was dead," Aunt Hope broke in.

"Do ye really think we'd kill yer dog, boy?" Aunt Veela asked almost gently, and I nodded stubbornly. "Well, I'll be a flop-eared jackass!" she roared, her pipe falling out of her mouth.

"One of you killed my dog," I said bitterly, "and in the worst way a body could. Ye'd've been a lot nicer iffen ye'd just shot him," I yelled, fully expecting one of the aunts to clobber me. And when none did, I went on, "I'm gonna find out who killed my dog iffen it takes the rest o' my life. An' iffen ye don't think I will, ye best tie me up in the barn or feed me ground glass in my taters or somethin'."

" 'By aunt or aunts unknown,' " Aunt Veela muttered. She sounded like she started to laugh and got choked on it. Then she said, "Boy, ye ought to know we wouldn't kill your dog, though he was the worst good-fer-nothin' dog I ever did see."

"Allus stealin' food," Aunt Hope said.

"And diggin' holes in my garden t' bury his bones," Aunt Faith added.

"See? Jest see? See how yer bad-mouthin' him?" I hissed, feeling rage nigh burn my ears off. "They ain't a one o' ye shed a tear, not a little bitty drop. Ye don't keer iffen he's dead. Ye don't keer 'cause ye killed him. An' jest maybe ye wont t' git rid o' me too."

"Now ye heer this, boy," Aunt Veela said, her voice stern. "That Hound Dog Bates was a no-good egg-suckin' thief. Sorriest dog I ever seen, bar none, an' 'tis a plain fact that we didn't like

19

him. Reckon ye could say we hated him. But none of us would have killed him, simply because he was yours. An' if the time comes that we wont t' git rid o' you, ye have my word I will give ye a head start." Then Aunt Veela snorted.

"I don't believe ye, Aunt Veela," I said, cold, right back. "It's my reckonin' one of ye went plumb crazy with dog hate an' killed my dog dead."

"Well, ye jest think whatever ye please," Aunt Veela said firmly. "As fer me, my bones is ready t' hit the bed."

"Ye tell him t' move that grave," Aunt Hope said shrilly, pointing a finger at me.

"Leave the boy be an' the grave," Aunt Veela said tiredly. "He'll find the truth one day."

Aunt Faith and Aunt Hope went in to do dishes, leaving me to sit on the porch staring at the faint outline of Hound Dog Bates's grave in the darkness.

CHAPTER 3

Things didn't work out the way I hoped they would.
I mean, I figured that when the aunts seen my
dog's grave, one of them would break down and
confess they killed him. But far as I could see, all
of them acted surprised that Hound Dog Bates
was dead. On the other hand, they might have
just been surprised that I'd buried him smack in
the middle of the yard.

I decided the only thing to do was find out all
I could about the aunts, one at a time. There had

to be a clue someplace that one of them had murder in her heart, 'less maybe all three of them had done it together, for I reckon they all hated him the same.

A big yellow-orange moon looking nigh hot as the sun came up over the hills, throwing the shadow of the cross on Hound Dog Bates's grave clear across the yard. A mockingbird that wasn't asleep made fun of other birds from the old snarled apple tree down near the pond. A deep loneliness rose up in me, not for Hound Dog Bates this time but for the aunts.

Truth to tell, I'd always liked them all right— till they'd killed my dog, I mean. They had raised me, and they were all the folks I had. But that didn't excuse them for killing my dog, I muttered, hardening myself for finding the murderer.

Somewhere far off a hound bayed at the moon, and it sounded so like Hound Dog Bates that my hair stood straight up on my head and fear crawled in goose bumps on my body, cooling it for the first time that day. The hound howled again, and in my mind I could see the ghost of Hound Dog Bates climbing a hill toward the orange-yellow moon.

As much as I loved my dog, I figured once he was dead and buried he ought to stay that way. I shot into the house to bed a little earlier and faster than I'd meant to. I slept lonely, ever reaching in my sleep to feel for Hound Dog Bates. I woke up in the morning thinking I'd never stop missing him.

Soon as I pulled my britches on, I ran outside to see if the grave was really there or if I'd been dreaming. It was there all right, and just under the cross at the head of the grave was three of Aunt Faith's yellow roses, her prize roses that she'd never let nobody but her touch. My eyes went even wider, for there was a small bunch of wild honeysuckle that was only living down nigh the dark cool of the spring where Aunt Hope went to gather her herbs, and a bunch of lacy ferns that only grew in the north forty so far away from the house that only Aunt Veela and me walked there.

I looked at the flowers, pondering that maybe all three of the aunts killed Hound Dog Bates and were trying to say they were sorry. Or two of them really were, and the third, the real killer, was just pretending and put the flowers there so I wouldn't know.

When I went in to breakfast, none of them looked sorry. They just looked like they always did. I mean to say they looked and ate as unconcerned as if I'd never had a dog and he wasn't buried smack dab in the middle of the pansy bed.

When I filled my plate, Aunt Veela said, "Boy, ye best help Hope can the 'maters today lest the sun rots them on the vine."

I just nodded. That suited me fine for it would give me a chance to get next to Aunt Hope and find out iffen she'd killed my dog. When Aunt Veela and Aunt Faith went out for their day's work, I even offered to wash dishes for Aunt Hope, nigh causing her to faint.

"No need, Sass," she said kindly. "Ye jest do yer barn work, then help me with the tomatoes."

By the time I got the barn in working order for the day, the sun was already beginning to scorch the earth and I figured all living things on it. I took baskets to the tomato field and started picking. I sorta wished I'd brought some salt, for I liked fresh tomatoes straight off the vine. Then decided they wouldn't taste good with my dog dead and gone. Then decided they would, 'cause it was my dog that was dead, not my belly. So when I took the first basket of tomatoes to the house, I brought salt back with me and ate the extra-juicy tomatoes till I was full.

I was glad school was out for the summer. It was too hot for the younguns who didn't have shoes to walk the long miles to school barefoot. On the other hand, it was too cold to walk to school in winter barefoot, so the little one-room school was closed most of the time.

One thing I could say for my aunts, they always bought me shoes come winter, even if they had to sell a pig or something to do it. Sometimes they had to talk long and hard about what we could do without that wouldn't hurt the most. And when they'd decided, they would put on their best clothes and go to the town seven miles away to find a buyer. Then there would be new shoes and overalls for me and something for Christmas.

'Course my feet grew real fast, so Aunt Faith or Aunt Hope would wear my outgrown shoes for work shoes when I couldn't fit in them any more.

I took the last basket of tomatoes to the house. Aunt Hope had the tub of water scalding hot to wash the fruit jars. Washing jars was my job 'cause I had the only hands small enough to get inside them. I helped her carry the tub of boiling water under the cottonwood tree in the backyard and started washing the jars in the strong lye soap. Aunt Hope squatted beside me, rinsing the clean jars in another tub.

I was never sure whether Aunt Hope's eyes were foggy-looking or just her glasses. I said, "Aunt Hope, how come you ain't married like other womenfolks?"

The jar she was holding slipped out of her hand under the boiling water and she had to fish it out with a stick. Then she looked at me with her foggy eyes and said, sorta proud-like, "I could've wed, Sass boy, more than once, I reckon," and her face went sorta dreamy, then stiff as she said, sharp-like, "and I reckon I ain't too old to wed yet, boy. I jest be thirty."

"But, Aunt Hope, why ain't ye married 'fore now?" I insisted.

" 'Cause they was too much t' do here," she said, harsh-like. "Ma was sick an' needed keer, an' then yore grandpa hurt his back in the log woods an' never could walk good agin. The years jest sorta slipped by, then you come along." She smiled at me.

"What was it like 'fore I come?" I asked, scrubbing last year's tomato stains on a fruit jar. "I mean, how was things when you were my age, Aunt Hope?"

Aunt Hope swished a fruit jar in the rinse water and said gently, her gaze far off, "Well, we was poor, Sass, poorer 'n now, but we didn't mind, not much, 'cause we had Pa an' then there was yer grandma. Ah, she was a sight, Sass, a pure sight. Her hair was gold, gold as yours, but her eyes was blue as the rain-washed April sky. She sang around the house and 'most danced at her chores, an' she kept us laughin' till we 'most never thought on bein' hungry.

"Veela an' Faith had it harder than me," Aunt Hope said sadly. "They had to work in the fields with Pa. An' me bein' the youngest, Ma kept me at the house t' help her work. Somehow, with Ma, work seemed more like play. Then when yer ma was born, yer Grandma only lived long enough t' name the baby Lovey. An' a love yer ma was, Sass, a spittin' image of yer grandma from the first.

"Pa sorta lost interest in livin' after Ma died, but Lovey an' young spirits kept me an' the other girls a-hoppin'. Yer ma was ever a free one, Sass, goin' at a dancin' run from the time she could walk, chasin' butterflies across the fields, chatterin' with the wild things in the woods.

"We girls had beaus then, Sass, an' the Jackson boy spoke for Veela, an' Faith had two or three a-sniffin' around her. Then somehow the years sorta slipped away an' the beaus with them. Reckon they wasn't o' mind t' wait till yer ma was grown. An' then a tree fell on Pa in the log woods. An' then, as I said, there was you, Sass."

Something deep inside me hurt, a deep lonesome hurt of lost years, and to keep from crying I said fast, "Maybe ye didn't wed because you didn't like dogs."

Aunt Hope raised her hand with a fruit jar in it and shook it at me, saying, "Sassafras Bates, I didn't kill yer blamed dog, though that dog orta've been killed when he was born. That dog was the dumbest, most aggravatin' critter ever birthed, an' ye ken bet yore britches I wonted t' kill him many a time but I didn't. Ye ort t' know I'd never kill no dog with ground glass. Now ye jest hesh an' tote those jars in the house."

Aunt Hope stomped off, and I was glad, for,

truth to tell, I thought she was gonna brain me with a fruit jar. I wished I hadn't made her mad, but figured she'd cool off and I could find out more about her. I figured she might have got so mad 'cause her conscience hurt, over killing my dog, I mean. And I didn't feel like crying any more.

By noon the hills were blazing hot and the kitchen hotter, and the whole world smelled of boiling tomatoes. When Aunt Faith and Aunt Veela came in for noon dinner, we sat under the cottonwood tree to eat sliced tomatoes, cucumbers, and drink cold buttermilk drawn up from its bucket hanging in the well. By the next month there would be ripe watermelons to cool in the spring below the house or in the dark cellar. Flies buzzed around our food and mouths, and Aunt Veela swatted at them angrily, but no one really complained, for there was no staying in the kitchen.

No one talked much, either, for the heat drained a body dry. All the aunts had tired lines on their faces. I felt sorrowful for them, but asked myself that if a man wasn't loyal to his own dog, who could he be loyal to? And he ought to find the murderer even if it was a tired-worn-out aunt.

The rest of the day was a blur of heat, sweat, and work. My nose was full of smelling tomato preserves, sweet and sticky. There were rows of them, some just plain tomatoes for cooking come winter, and other jars of small green pickled ones. It seemed strange that a body worked and sweated themselves nigh to death in hot summer in order to live in the blue-cold winter.

Along toward evening Aunt Hope said tiredly but kindly, "Sass, yer a big help, boy, an' iffen ye'll fill the woodbox an' water buckets, I reckon I best git the week's bread baked while the stove is so hot."

She kept wiping her red face with her apron to keep the sweat out of her eyes. I was glad to get outside, though it wasn't much cooler, and I reckoned Aunt Hope wasn't mad at me no more. I filled the water pails and the woodbox and did my barn chores. The smell of new bread baking took the place of tomatoes, and there was gingerbread, too.

As we sat down to eat, Aunt Veela said, "Shorely t' goodness this heer weather will break afore long. Iffen it don't, it will be a tornado fer shore."

Aunt Faith said, "I ain't never in my born days seen hot weather like this break without a bad storm."

After supper we all helped clear the boiling kitchen and headed for the porch. We'd no more than sat down when Aunt Hope stared at the dog's grave and burst out crying, scaring my neck hairs stiff 'cause I'd never seen her cry afore. She jumped up and ran in the house, and Aunt Veela turned pure ice eyes on me, saying, "Sass, yer Aunt Hope is a plumb tender person, an' that fool of a dog's grave under her nose is liable t' break her down."

I stared cold as I could right back at Aunt Veela, but my insides were jumping nine to the dozen. I wasn't sure that what I was thinking was right. I mean, I'd heerd that women without menfolks was sort of addled, leastways Eddie Lee Horton said old-maid women went crazy when they never wed. He said it in school once. Said I'd be crazy, too, 'cause of crazy women raising me. 'Course I had to whop him for calling my aunts crazy, and even if he said it now, I'd have to whop him again. But I wasn't real sure he wasn't right—I mean, never having been around womenfolks with men.

I was glad when Aunt Veela gave a tired sigh and looked away from me, for right at the moment there was a deep fear in me that them women was plumb tired of working to take care of me. And I'd have bet a bedbug to a toad frog that before long I'd be murdered dead as Hound Dog Bates. And it wouldn't surprise me none iffen they didn't bury me smack in the middle of the yard, maybe right in the middle of the pansy bed beside Hound Dog Bates.

I couldn't really blame them. I mean, I'd blame the dickens out of them for killing me, but I didn't blame them for being tired of raising me. Truth to tell, I'd have got tired of working and raising a body long afore they was twelve years old. And since I figured they was gonna kill me anyway, I decided to sneak a piece of the cake Aunt Hope had made but not cut yet. I mean, after all, a body could be killed only once.

CHAPTER 4

At breakfast no one mentioned the cake, and Aunt Veela said, "Sass, since all of them overripe 'maters has been canned, I reckon ye ken go fer a swim in Big Creek after the barn chores is done."

I didn't know what to say except just nodding thank-you. Then, narrowing my eyes, I looked hard at the women, thinking maybe they were trying to get me out of the way so they could plan my killing. 'Course my aunts had let me go swimming before in hot weather and never killed me, but that was before Hound Dog Bates was murdered, and I never suspected them of nothing then.

"Don't glare them brown eyes at me," Aunt Faith said. I looked down at my plate so they wouldn't think I knowed nothing.

I pushed my straw-colored hair out of my eyes. Seemed it was always too long, for Aunt Veela never had time to cut it much. I took a last swipe at my plate with a biscuit, and, avoiding Aunt Hope's red-rimmed eyes, I headed for the barn chores, sorta hoping Aunt Hope wasn't the murderer. On the other hand, I didn't want none of them to be it. "But it had t' be them," I muttered to myself, " 'cause they was the only ones livin' here 'sides me, an' I wouldn't kill my own dog."

I made short work of the barn and chicken house. Then I stopped at the house just long enough to pick up a pail of lunch that Aunt Hope always sent with me for a day of swimming.

The sun was hot even before it was up good, and I could feel it on my bare shoulders. I hadn't bothered putting on another shirt since I'd buried Hound Dog Bates in my best. I wished I lived in the woods by myself and I'd go plumb naked.

The path to the big creek was near the north

forty, so I decided to stop by and talk to Aunt Veela, though truth to tell I was sorta scared to be with Aunt Veela so far from the others. Fact of the matter was, the north forty was a good place to get rid of most anything.

The field smelled of new-turned earth, and the hills echoed with Aunt Veela's yelling at ol' Sauce. I stopped at the edge of the field to watch Aunt Veela guide the plow and nigh jumped over myself when a sluggish rattlesnake came wiggling out of the new-plowed ground at my feet. Aunt Veela had dug up its hole with the plow.

I climbed up on the fence to wait for Aunt Veela to come back my way. I nearly laughed out loud when Aunt Veela screamed, "Sauce, ye flop-eared jackass, git a move on! *Gee! Gee! Haw!* Ye ol' buzzard-bait, move!" I wondered how mules knew that "gee" meant for them to turn right and "haw" meant for them to turn left, but they did know and turned where commanded.

At the end of the long row Aunt Veela saw me and yelled, "Anything the matter, Sass?"

"No, jist wanted to talk with ye a mite," I yelled back, and watched her and the mule plod toward me.

For the first time I noticed that Aunt Veela looked small behind the huge mule, wearing Grandpa's too-big britches and the old floppy hat that kept falling over her ears. Black gnats hovered around her and the mule, and I figgered maybe they made Aunt Veela sharp-tongued and mean. I knew for a fact that black gnats could 'most make a preacher cuss.

At the end of the row ol' Sauce dropped his head to nibble at the dry grass. Aunt Veela leaned on the plow handles, taking off the hat to wipe sweat from her face, and asked, "Now what ye want, Sass?"

"I jist—uh—well, I sorta wanted to know why ye never wed, Aunt Veela."

Aunt Veela snorted and said, "Really, Sass, I never had the time." Then, kinda grinning, she said she never found a man as smart as ol' Sauce.

"What was it like when you were my age, Aunt Veela?"

"A lot like it is now, I reckon," Aunt Veela said, leaning harder on the plow, " 'cept we got more to eat now, and there's hope that someday we might have a tractor, before I get too old to cuss Sauce. Be a lot easier on these old bones,"

Aunt Veela said 'most to herself. Then she looked me straight in the eye and asked, "Ye still think I killed your dog, boy?"

I leaped over the fence away from her, saying fast, "I gotta go now," leaving her to stare after me. The trail through the woods to Big Creek was grown up with dog fennel, and I stepped high and careful, 'cause when the weather got this hot, snakes got mad as hops and would strike at 'most anything. Another thing that made them mad was losing their skins, and I seen two empty skins even before I got to the bend in the trail. Even though I'd lived around snakes all my life, they was apt to make me jumpy in hot weather. Black gnats started flying around my face 'cause they like sweat and there was enough on my face to drown them. As bad as I dreaded summer storms, I wished we'd have one, a drenching rain and cracking thunder to clear the air.

I turned my head, even had my mouth open to call Hound Dog Bates, when I realized that he'd never come to my call again, not that he ever came to my call before, 'less he wanted to. But a deep lonesome started at my toes and seemed to hurt even my ears. So no matter it was so hot, I

started to run. I had to run to keep from screaming like a gut-shot panther. I jumped old rotten
logs, ducked low-growing tree branches, and come
nigh braining myself on a hard maple.

I could smell the coolness of the creek before I
seen it, and I started slipping out of my overalls.
The last few yards I ran buck-naked, stopping long
enough to hang my lunch bucket on a limb. I dove
off the bank into the clear deep water, splashing
and screeching till my lonesome went away.

I flipped over on my back and floated. The grass
around the streambed was new-green-looking,
even crisper than the leaf lettuce that Aunt Faith
grew in the garden. I flipped on my stomach and
watched orange crawdads and black tadpoles
splash by under me. And next to the white gravel
floor of the streambed, goldfish swam in schools.
A big catfish darted under a large rock, scared off
by my shadow, I reckon.

Suddenly the whole stream and hills seemed to
break open, and I nigh drowned myself when a
man's voice roared, "Hey, boy! Since ye scared
off all the damn fish, come talk t' me."

I nose-dived under the water and came up
choking and sputtering, shaking the water and wet

hair out of my eyes. When I could see, I seen the biggest man I'd ever seen sitting beside the trunk of an old tree. I never knew of anybody but me using this part of the creek afore.

I stumbled up on the bank and pulled my overalls on, eyeing the man. He had a wide grin, big as a water bucket, seemed to me. Fact, everything about him was big—his bright blue eyes, his large fat eyebrows. And they was colored real cheerful. I mean, his hair and eyebrows were sorta different colors, all happy-looking, gold and brown and reddish. His teeth were large and square, and his hands and feet looked nigh as big as my whole body, and when he stood up, and up, and up, I thought he was going to raise high as the old oak tree.

He wore bib overalls like me, only his would have fit a covered wagon, I reckon. But there wasn't no fat on him that I could see.

"Put her thar, boy," he said, thrusting out a hand that mine was lost in. "I'm Kelly O'Kelly. What's yore handle?"

"Sassafras Bates," I said, standing as tall as I could. "But folks call me Sass."

"Well, boy, folks call me Kelly." He grinned

and sat down on the bank of the creek.

I dropped down facing him, saying, "Mr. Kelly, I ain't never seen nobody fish here 'fore 'cept me. Whar ye from?"

"I'm from the highways an' the byways, Sass, my boy. I have wandered hither an' yon an' to an' fro across the land, but when I seen these hills, I knew I'd come home." His voice grew soft and dreamy.

And I was in another world as he told me about cities I'd never heard of before, hot dirty cattle yards, and whole families living in two rooms. I could smell diapers and boiling cabbage and hear the whimper of the too-crowded children and look down into hard pavement below covered with trash and garbage. And as the hours passed, he told me about a place called Ireland and a big ship that brought him and his family across the sea to America. And he told me about working in steel mills till he got enough money to buy him a place, and about how he'd wandered about, bumming rides on freight trains till he got to Arkansas and knew he was home. And I couldn't believe it. He wanted to live right here in the hills, and I hoped fierce that he would.

I got the lunch bucket off the tree limb, and my eyes popped when he put a whole biscuit in his mouth at once. It was such a wondrous sight, watching him eat, that I let him eat all the food and just came back to earth when he said, "Boy, yer mother makes the best biscuits I ever ate."

"Ain't my ma's cooking," I said. "My ma's dead. I live with my old-maid aunts. Aunt Hope, the youngest, is the cook."

"How old is yore aunt, Sass?"

"Younger than you are, I reckon," for he looked not as old as Aunt Faith, but not as young as Aunt Hope.

"Yore aunts like company, boy?"

"Don't know," I said, " 'cause we don't have much." And with his questioning me, I told him how my pa left and Grandpa died and how my aunts ran the farm. I couldn't figure why in the world he wanted to know, but when he asked, I told him the best I could how the aunts looked. "How come you want to know?" I finally asked curiously.

"Lookin' fer a wife, boy," he said. "Don't have t' be too much on looks, but has t' be a lot on cook." Then he threw back his head and made the hills shake with his laughing. For no reason I knowed, I laughed too, loud as I could, and it was a strange good feeling 'cause I never remembered laughing big, out loud before.

I didn't come to myself till he said, "Well, boy, will ye invite me t' supper?"

All my fear came back, and I looked him straight in the eye and said bitterly, "Well, Mr. Kelly O'Kelly, yer right welcome by me t' come t' supper, but ye'll jest have t' take yer chance on bein' murdered same as me."

CHAPTER 5

Mr. Kelly O'Kelly's eyes bugged at me, and he said,
"Ye mean that, boy? Ye mean there's a murderer
at yer house?"

"I ought t' know. I ain't lyin', mister, 'cause I
found his body, an' all three of my aunts hated
him like pizen."

Mr. Kelly squatted, bringing his face level with
mine, saying, "When did this murder take place,
son?"

"Day before yesterday."

"Who was killed, boy?"

"My best friend."

Mr. Kelly put his big hand on my shoulder gently, saying, "Are you sure he was dead, boy?"

"Ought t' know, mister, 'cause it was me who buried him."

Muttering stuff about saints and things I'd never heard of before, though it sorta sounded like praying folks did in church, only a different way, Mr. Kelly finally muttered, "Well, if the poor person wasn't dead, he's bound t' be by now." Straightening up, he said, "Where did you bury the body, boy?"

"Smack dab in the middle of Aunt Faith's pansy bed. Smack dab in the middle of the yard where the killer has t' look at her dirty work every time she steps out the door. Ye see, Mr. Kelly, I figgered iffen the womenfolks seen the grave they'd confess, but they didn't. Aunt Hope cried. She's the one who baked the biscuits ye ate, but she didn't confess."

"Well, boy, in a way you were smart t' think the grave might make them confess. On the other hand, you were dumb because the one who killed yer friend might try t' knock ye off, too."

"I know that, mister. That's why I told ye ye'd have t' take yer chances on a-gettin' killed deader 'n a doornail along with me. 'Cause I figger if they put ground glass in the food, it'll git both of us."

"Ground glass?"

"Yes, Mr. Kelly, that's what killed the best friend I ever had."

"Wicked cruel," Mr. Kelly muttered. Then, looking at me, his happy look gone, he said, "Boy, now ye keep this under yer hat, but I was on the police force in Chicago for a few years before I started my wandering. And I know something about catchin' killers. Tell ye what. I'll pretend I'm out of work and offer to work for your aunts for room and board. That way I can sorta keep an eye on you."

"Mister, that would be a plumb relief," I said sincerely.

We walked on toward home, me taking ten steps, seemed to me, to his one.

As we walked along, Mr. Kelly asked me stuff about the aunts. "How come yer aunts hated yer friend, Sass?" he asked.

"For different reasons," I said, suddenly feeling I ought to be fair to my aunts. "I reckon, mister, that truth t' tell they did have reasons. Aunt Hope hated him 'cause he was a mite greedy. I mean, if he couldn't beg the last piece o' cake or chicken, he was apt t' steal it. Fact of the matter, it might have been fast kidneys that got him killed. None of the aunts could abide him a-peein' in the house."

"Pore ol' soul," Mr. Kelly muttered, then added, " 'Most all old folks lose control of their kidneys after a certain age."

" 'Twasn't age with him, mister. Truth t' tell, he sorta liked t' make the aunts mad. I mean, long as he could dodge Aunt Hope's broom and run faster than any of them."

Looking puzzled, Mr. Kelly asked, "Ain't ye got a bathroom?"

"Not in the house," I said. "The town ain't put plumbin' out fer as we live."

"Well, boy, I'm right sorry yore friend's gone, an' in such a dreadful way. An' t' be honest with ye, I cain't say I wouldn't wont t' kill somebody if they deliberately peed on furniture an' stuff. An' t' be more honest, I think yer friend was a mite touched. But still, murder is murder an' it's wrong no matter how it's done or what causes it. Are ye right shore yer aunts done it?"

"Well, Aunt Faith said he messed up her garden, and Aunt Veela, who bosses all of us, said he was jest plumb no good fer nothin'."

"Do ye think yer aunts will need a work hand, boy?"

"Hard as they work, mister, they could use a dozen, but our farm is pore as the other dirt farms around, so they ain't never got no money t' pay fer work. Fact is, my aunts allus have t' sell somethin' we need t' buy my winter shoes."

"If yer that pore, maybe there won't be enough fer me."

"Oh, there's plenty o' food, Mr. Kelly—I mean in summer leastways—'cause we spend most of our time raisin' an' cannin' it. 'Sides, the woods is full o' wild fruit an' the creek banks thick with berries, an' Aunt Hope keeps me hoppin', gatherin' it all t' can."

We walked slow, and I told him how Aunt Veela sorta bossed us all 'cause she done the hardest farming, and about Aunt Faith doing the garden and yard work. But he seemed most interested in Aunt Hope 'cause she done the cooking, or was the youngest one. I reckon he was just joking

about wanting a wife, or if he wasn't joking before, I knowed he wouldn't want one of the aunts
for a wife now that he knew she could very well
be a murderer.

The swim in the creek had cooled me off for the
first time since summer started, but by the time
we got to the house, I was sweating hot again.

"We'd best go in the back way," I said, " 'cause
Aunt Hope likes menfolks t' be clean when they
come in her kitchen."

We stopped at the well to draw up water to
drink and wash our hands and faces. Mr. Kelly
took his hat off before stepping after me in the
door. Aunt Hope was stirring a pot of beans at
the stove, and hearing us, she looked up and gave
a scream, dropping her spoon.

"It's all right, Aunt Hope," I said fast-like. "This
is Mr. Kelly O'Kelly. He's come to eat supper with
us."

Mr. Kelly grinned real big at Aunt Hope, and
she sorta pushed her hair around nervous-like, and
Mr. Kelly said, "Boy, is this heer the aunt that
makes them delicious biscuits?"

I nodded, and he said, "I met the boy while I
was fishin', an' he shared his lunch, an' t' tell ye

the truth, madam, I'd have walked a hundred miles t' taste food that good agin."

"Do declare. Do declare," Aunt Hope kept saying, looking pleased and not pleased at the same time.

I said, "Well, I'd best git the barn chores done," and Mr. Kelly said, "I'll help ye, boy," and went out the door first.

Aunt Hope dragged my overall straps, saying, "Boy, now how dast ye bring company when I ain't got no company vittles fixed?" and I could have swore she looked at me just like she used to look at Hound Dog Bates, and I was glad Mr. Kelly had come.

"Mr. Kelly won't keer that it ain't company vittles, Aunt Hope," I said. "All he keers is jest fer lots of it."

Aunt Hope let me go, and I shot out the door before she could collar me again. Mr. Kelly was like me. I mean, it didn't make him wrinkle up his nose, cleaning barn stalls and feeding hogs. He was good to work with in other ways, too, 'cause he whistled real cheerful. And I figured I could get to like him 'most as good as Hound Dog Bates. But reckoned I'd best hold off with my feelings in case he got killed, too.

There might not have been company vittles when we came home, but when we came in from cleaning the barn, there sure was. Aunt Hope was all dressed up sorta pretty, too, except for sweat running off her. But then it was running off us all.

Mr. Kelly seemed to fill up the whole kitchen, making my aunts look littler than they were. And suddenly it was like we were having a party or what I thought a party was like, 'cause I'd never been to one. I didn't even mind the heat for a change.

Mr. Kelly's laughter boomed, and he talked garden to Aunt Faith and man-to-man crops with Aunt Veela. Not that she was a man, of course—I mean, he just treated her like she had the good sense that she did have about farming. But it was Aunt Hope who looked all flustered and the happiest, 'cause Mr. Kelly ate huge helpings and bragged on her cooking every plateful. And it did seem she'd outdone herself. Besides the big pot of pinto beans full of bacon chunks, there was fried potatoes, corn bread, young ears of yellow corn, a big platter of sliced fresh tomatoes, green onions, radishes, lettuce mixed with small mustard greens, coffee, buttermilk, and a big bowlful of butter. And to top it off, there were strawberries, the very last from out of Aunt Faith's garden, to eat with the yellow egg cake and cream.

From the way Mr. Kelly put the food away, I figured there wasn't nothing in it—I mean, like ground glass or poison, 'cause Mr. Kelly had been a policeman and he'd know. So I dug in, too, the hungriest I'd been since finding Hound Dog Bates.

After supper Mr. Kelly insisted on helping clean up the kitchen with the rest of us. Then he followed us to the porch, sitting beside me, and lit up a black cigar and lit Aunt Veela's pipe for her. In the ruckus of getting settled in their rockers, Mr. Kelly whispered, "That yer friend's grave?"

I nodded yes, and he walked over to look. He was so still in the evening dusk, his head bowed over the cross, that it sorta scared me. I went over to him and nigh fainted for his body was shaking like he was having a fit. His eyes looked all crinkly cheerful-like, but I knowed better 'cause tears was running down his cheeks. I reached up and put my hand in his 'cause I knew I'd found a friend for life. I mean, him a-loving dogs so much he could cry over a strange one. I mean, he didn't even know Hound Dog Bates.

CHAPTER 6

All evening seemed like a party, right up to the time Aunt Veela made me go to bed. Mr. Kelly was asked to share the screened-in back porch with me. When I awoke the next morning, the old iron bedstead from the barn loft was set up across from my bed, and Mr. Kelly was rocking the porch with the loudest snores I'd ever heard.

I knew without asking him that Aunt Veela had worked out the room-and-board thing, and truth to tell, it made me feel sorta bad. I mean, Aunt

Veela and them having a person spy on them, only not knowing it. But a body hadn't ought to mess with a man's dog in hound dog country.

As soon as I got up, I knew there wasn't going to be any learning secrets from Aunt Hope, 'cause she was wearing her best dress, the one with the blue flowers, and she was humming as she piled the table with fresh-churned butter, tomato preserves, peach butter, fried eggs, and a platter of the cured ham she was usually so careful with.

I wondered why Aunt Hope was acting so pert-like. I mean, Mr. Kelly was my friend, but maybe she thought he was hers, too. But I knowed he liked her just 'cause of her cooking.

With Mr. Kelly there, even breakfast seemed like a happy time. The rest of us was usually grumpy in the early morning. He bragged on the biscuits and told Aunt Hope the blue flowers in her dress matched her eyes, and looking at her, her eyes did seem bright, the fog sorta gone out of them. Even Aunt Veela and Aunt Faith strutted a mite when he told them what a good job they'd done on the farm.

But it puzzled me how Aunt Veela and Aunt Faith gave Aunt Hope sorta sour looks when Mr.

Kelly wasn't looking, and I figured all of them wanted him for a special friend by themselves. Of course, he was mine, sorta like Hound Dog Bates, only a lot bigger.

After we ate, Mr. Kelly said he'd catch the mail car to town and pick up his things at the boardinghouse where he'd been staying and come back that evening in time for supper.

He grinned at Aunt Hope, and then he said, "Come walk me to the highway, boy." And I was glad to. I mean, he might make the womenfolks feel good and kinda fluttery, but me and him was menfolks, sort of a tie between us, like cleaning barn stalls without getting queasy.

As we strolled down the hill to the old hard-dirt road, the sun came up quickly, taking away what little coolness the night had left. I felt sweat break out on me and could see it starting to darken Mr. Kelly's overalls. But he didn't seem to mind. He was puffing on another black cigar, not saying nothing. So I tried to keep up with him, watching him to see what he had to say. When we turned the bend in the road by the pond, he said softly, "Sass, ye have any new folks move in around here lately?"

"No. I mean, all the folks I know been here all their lives."

"No new folks at all, eh?"

"No, 'cept maybe Mr. Watts's boy Clem. But he belongs here. He went away 'fore I was born an' come back a few months ago t' take over the farm when his pa died. I think maybe him an' Aunt Faith was sorta sweet on each other when they was younguns 'cause Aunt Hope an' Aunt Veela teased her about her ol' beau comin' home, but Aunt Faith got mad an' they hushed. Mr. Kelly, are ye tryin' t' say ye don't think my aunts kilt Hound Dog Bates?"

"Now, I'm not a-sayin' nothin', boy, jest that a good detective looks at a case from all sides of the matter, gatherin' clues an' so forth before steppin' in for the arrest. A man has t' keep his head, ye know."

"Yes." I nodded. I could see the sense in that, and there wasn't nothing I'd like better than finding my aunts not guilty. 'Cause it was a plain fact, if they didn't kill Hound Dog Bates, they wouldn't kill me. So I said, "Well, I reckon I'll sorta nose around a mite, though I still think we'll find the killer close t' home."

"Don't count on it, boy," Mr. Kelly said. "Yore aunts are real nice-actin' ladies."

"Ladies!" I looked at him, my eyes nigh popping. "Why, mercy above, Mr. Kelly, them aunts o' mine would sour cider vinegar, they's so sharp at times."

"Maybe they have reason t' be sharp, boy."

"Ye goin' back on me, Mr. Kelly?"

"No, boy, I'm not. Jest sayin' don't be sure of nothin' till it's proved."

We came back to the road, and Mr. Kelly waved a big hand at me. I walked back up the hill slowly, thinking Mr. Kelly just didn't know them old aunts good as me. Just wait till he done something they didn't like, like tracking mud in the kitchen or getting him a dog, I thought, and he'd see how soon the sharp tongues turned on him.

After I did the barn chores, I hung around the kitchen for a spell, for the whole house smelled like Christmas—in the middle of July, too. Apple pies lined the shelf next to the well, cooling, their crusts all brown and bubbly with butter, brown sugar, and cinnamon. Aunt Hope was plucking frying chickens, sweat dripping off her chin. When she caught me eating green beans out of the pot on the stove with my fingers, she said sharp as could be, "Sass, ye git outta that kitchen till dinnertime. An' don't ye eat outta pots with yer dirty fingers."

I left, but I left thinking, I wish Mr. Kelly could hear that kind of talk and he wouldn't think Aunt Hope so sweet, though I bet myself she'd get all honey pie when he came back. 'Course him being an ex-policeman, he could probably see through their sweet put-ons all right.

Feeling better and worse at the same time, 'cause there was times when I liked my aunts, I decided to go help Aunt Faith and find out about Clem Watts. Aunt Faith was kneeling beside a row of runner beans, tying them to poles, and she looked surprised when I dropped down beside her, saying, "Ye need any help?"

Her black eyes looked like they was laughing, but her voice was sharp as always when she said dryly, "Well, I'd druther know what ye wont, Sass."

I could feel my face turn red for being found out so easy, but I said anyway, "Aunt Faith, was Clem Watts really yer beau years an' years an' years an' years ago?"

Looking puzzled, Aunt Faith turned a bean vine over in her fingers, saying, "Well, he weren't no more my beau than Veela's." Then she laughed. "But neither Veela nor me knowed he was the other's beau. An' I reckon he was courtin' half the women in the country 'sides us. Reckon he was allus a sly one."

"How come he left here?"

"Well"—Aunt Faith sorta grinned, the freckles shining on her nose—"iffen ye had most o' the women in the hills after ye, wouldn't ye leave t' save yer hide?"

"In one hop an' a jump." I laughed back at Aunt Faith, and it was a strange thing. I mean, laughing with each other. I reckon Mr. Kelly had brought laughing with him, and, dog killers or not, I sure hoped the laughing stayed.

I pulled a handful of weeds and said, "What was it like when you was a youngun, Aunt Faith?"

" 'Twas a good life fer me," Aunt Faith said, thoughtfully rolling a plump green bean in her fingers. " 'Course I was allus crazy fer the land. Liked the feel o' dirt 'twixt my fingers an' toes. Reckon it was hard on Veela an' Hope, though. We was mighty pore, boy, but a body cain't feel pore with God's green earth underfoot and the blue sky overhead and the smell of growing things in the air."

"How come ye didn't wed?" I asked, remembering how Aunt Hope said menfolks wouldn't wait for them. But Aunt Faith laughed lightly, saying, "Maybe I never found a man I liked more than dirt diggin'." Then she surprised me with the bitterness in her voice when she said, "Looks like it ain't too late fer Hope, after all."

"If ye mean Mr. Kelly, he's *my* friend," I protested, and Aunt Faith's face went all soft, and she said gently, "I'm glad fer ye, Sass, an' Hope too. Maybe I'm gettin' old."

"No, ye ain't, Aunt Faith. Ye ain't gettin' old at all," I said firmly, but truth to tell, I thought she was old, real, real old. So I wandered away from the garden and walked down the road, and it wasn't till I was in the place in the road where I'd found Hound Dog Bates that I knew I'd decided to go see Clem Watts. I mean, Mr. Kelly would expect me to check out everybody around, I reckon, the way a good detective would.

Finding Mr. Kelly had sorta filled up part of the empty spot inside me that Hound Dog Bates had left. But I was determined as ever to find his killer and let the ax of guilt fall where it may. I thought grimly of the aunts. I just had to quit feeling sorry for them. Maybe they wanted me to. I mean, maybe they wanted me to feel sorry for them so I wouldn't suspect, then they'd wham me deader than a squashed toad frog.

It was only about a mile to the old run-down Watts place, but the heat of the road made me jump like a flea on a mad dog, leaping from shade to shade and running on my toes where there was none. Black gnats fogged around my face, and I figured them little buggers would drive me plumb crazy, and I hated them fierce. They went and got in my eyes and flew up my nose, and I bet I swallowed a hundred and eighty-three in this summer alone. I stared at the sky, but it was still yellow-orange, no clouds at all.

The Watts place was more run-down than ours, and I reckon that was saying a lot. The yard was grown up with weeds. There was hickory and black walnut trees in the yard, and last year's nuts stained the ground with their hulls. A tall thin man, half bald, sat on the porch in a broken-down chair, spitting tobacco juice at a lizard sunning himself on the fence. Truth to tell, the man could spit better than anybody I'd ever seen, and Arkansas was plumb full of good tobacco spitters.

The man stared at me with eyes as hooded and small and cold as the lizard's. A chill started crawling up my backbone, and I stared back at the man, saying, "Howdy! Ye be Clem Watts?"

"Mebbe I is an' mebbe I ain't," the man said, spitting at the lizard again. "Who wonts t' know?"

"I do," I said, cool as I could.

"Well, who ye be?"

"Sassafras Bates. Ye be Clem Watts or not?"

"Reckon I am. What d'ye wont?"

"Jest come t' be neighborly."

"Don't wont no company," he said, spitting again.

"Well, looks like ye got some anyway," I said firm, but wanting to run.

"Whar ye belong at, boy?"

"Live with my aunts, Hope, Veela, and Faith."

"Them women still around?" he asked, jerking up straight.

"Yes, they're my aunts."

"Well, well," Clem said, and I didn't like the look in his beady eyes. "Them women's all wed up, I reckon," he stated, making it sound like a question.

I felt like saying, yes, and they got real big husbands, but then thought maybe if he come to call on my aunts, Mr. Kelly could spy on him better. So I said, "No, they ain't wed. But they could be," I went on, not wanting him to think they cared for the likes of him. Fact of the matter, it was beyond me why the aunts let him court them atall, so I said, "They got beaus by the dozen, but fer some reason they don't never wed none o' them. Fact of the matter, mister, more than a few men killed themselves dead 'cause o' my aunts turning them flat down."

Then I wished I hadn't mentioned killing, but reckon he never heard, 'cause he said, "I reckon they'd all be dried up an' turned t' vinegar by now." Clem sorta snickered, and a caring for my aunts came up in me from a place deep inside I didn't know I had.

"Ye be a plumb addled skunk iffen ye think that," I snapped, " 'cause all the menfolks in these hills says my aunts is plumb beautiful. An' iffen ye don't believe me, ye jest come t' supper tonight."

It was a dare I was hoping and praying he wouldn't take, but that bugger just smiled mean as a rattlesnake and said, "I'll be thar, boy." And my heart fell to my toes and, looking up at the sun, I knowed I just had a few hours to get home and make my aunts beautiful. And only the good Lord knowed how I was going to do it.

I ran toward home, figuring I'd die of sunstroke. But it wasn't even noon when I got back. I sat on the porch, letting some of the heat run out of me, 'fore facing the aunts at noon dinner.

If I was expecting fried chicken and apple pie, I was sure wrong, 'cause Aunt Hope said bashfully that all the stuff was for supper when Mr. Kelly got back. Aunt Veela and Aunt Faith looked at each other with a ain't-that-just-like-Hope look. Then they looked down at their plates, shamedlike.

I said, louder than I meant, "Well, we got more company comin' fer supper."

"Who in the world!" Aunt Faith stuttered.

Swallowing a lump in my gizzard, I said straight to Aunt Veela, "Will ye please hear me out 'fore ye say anything?" or kill me, I added to myself. "Now ye know, Aunt Veela, I don't ask fer much, an' jest this once please don't talk till I finish."

"All right, Sass boy, say yore piece," Aunt Veela

said, laying down her fork. She waited, and so did the others.

"Well, ye see, Aunt Veela, I sorta run int' Clem Watts t'day." There were gasps from Aunt Hope and Aunt Faith, but Aunt Veela frowned them quiet, and I went on. "Well, I mean to say I sorta run int' him on his front porch. An' he wonted t' know if ye be wed, an' I said no, but the hills was workin' alive with beaus a-pinin' fer ye. An' he said he bet you were dried up an' turned t' vinegar. An' I said no, you was the most beautiful women ever in these hills. An' he sorta didn't believe me, so I said come t' supper."

The words gushed out of me, but Aunt Veela never batted an eye, so I went on. "So, Aunt Veela, will ye please wear a dress, an', Aunt Faith, ye fix yore hair." I stuttered to a stop and to dead silence, figuring I didn't have to worry about ground glass in my food any more, for the way them women were staring at me I reckoned to get skinned alive with a dull knife.

CHAPTER 7

To my surprise, not to say nigh heart failure, Aunt Veela leaned back in her chair and howled with laughter. Then Aunt Faith got a dose of giggles, and I just sat staring, bug-eyed. When she could stop laughing, Aunt Veela said, "Ye know, Faith, I've allus hoped fer a chance t' git back at that Clem Watts fer his sneaky ways. Ye game, Faith?"

"I'd jest shorely love to." Aunt Faith giggled.

Then Aunt Veela said, "Boy, I reckon this heer farm ain't gonna fall fer a-missin' half a day's work. 'Sides, that mountain of a man Mr. Kelly will be helpin' us with the work. So ye git busy an' draw up the washtub o' water t' heat. Me an' Faith's got us some bathin' an' hair washin' t' do. Hope, ye git a-crackin' on the best supper ye ever cooked iffen it takes all our egg money, an' send the boy t' the crossroads store fer whatever ye need. An', Sass, after ye git the water drawed, ye go t' the store fer yer aunt an' sorta stay outta our way fer a spell."

I nodded and went to draw up the water. When I'd finished, Aunt Hope gave me five dollars and said I could have twenty-five cents for a jawbreaker. She wanted vanilla flavoring, a box of sage leaves, and ribbon, she said, a yard of blue, a yard of yellow, and a yard of green. I hotfooted it to the crossroads store, figuring sure that somebody was going to find me just a greasy spot in the road where I'd fried to death. And before I got there I wondered a hundred times if a jawbreaker and ribbons were worth it.

Mr. Jackson at the crossroads store said anybody fool enough to come out in the heat deserved a free jawbreaker and a cold bottle of strawberry pop. I thanked him for the pop and drank it while he measured ribbon, and I bought another jawbreaker with the twenty-five cents Aunt Hope said I could have.

I liked our small general store much better than those big supermarkets in town. I liked to walk around, seeing and smelling and touching. It was kind of dark and cool, with pine floors. Hickory-smoked sides of bacon hung from hooks, along with pink hams and strings of onion and red pepper. Huge dill pickles floated in a brine barrel, and stiff new overalls filled one shelf. I reckoned our store hadn't changed in a hundred years, for mule harnesses still hung on the walls. I felt like just staying there out of the hot glare of the sun.

I left the store looking like I had mumps in both jaws. Sucking on the candy helped make the trip home go a lot faster, it seemed to me. I came home to splashing and giggling. Aunt Hope met me at the back door and took the package and said, "Sass, ye git in the shade someplace an' cool off. Yer aunts will be a spell yet."

Truth to tell, I didn't have much hope of the aunts ever looking even fair-to-middlin', let alone beautiful, but I figured if they was ugly as mud fences they'd beat ol' Clem Watts a mile.

I sat under the oak till the sun started down, thinking maybe if the aunts had had a man around to make them as happy as Mr. Kelly made them, they wouldn't have killed Hound Dog Bates. I went and done the barn chores, then washed up at the well.

"Ye ken come in now, Sass," Aunt Hope called.

I stepped in the door, then stopped like I'd been pole-axed, for the aunts standing for me to look at looked like three winter-dried flowers come to life with spring newness. My mouth opened and I couldn't get nothing out. Aunt Hope had her hair in curls tied up with the blue ribbon. Aunt Veela's red curls were tied with the green ribbon, and the yellow one made Aunt Faith's hair look black as coal. Their eyelashes had suddenly grown long and dark, and their lips and cheeks had turned red as the rose growing in the corner of the picket fence. And they was beautiful, and my voice came out in, "Yer jest beautiful. Yer as beautiful as I told Clem Watts ye was."

"Mr. Watts t' ye, boy," Aunt Hope said.

"But I don't like him," I protested.

"Not likin' is no excuse fer bad manners, boy," Aunt Faith said, so I nodded but didn't feel no different about Clem Watts. Aunt Faith and Aunt Veela giggled like girls and didn't seem sour at Aunt Hope any more.

The kitchen smelled pure eating good. Instead of two frying chickens, there was now four, all brown, baked whole with sage and onion dressing. There was an old yellow tablecloth on the table and two coal oil lamps instead of one. My aunts might hardly never, ever do nothing, but when they did, they sure done it good, I thought, for I'd never seen a cloth on the table except the oilcloth.

I could hear Mr. Kelly whistling clear from the mail car stop on the road below the house, and Aunt Hope fluttered around making sure all was ready. I could smell buttermilk biscuits, and there was the bowl of butter to go with them. There was cranberry jelly and pickled tomatoes, chow-chow, and bread-and-butter pickles, a steaming platter of fried corn and a bowl of smashed 'taters with butter running in little yellow streams down the side. There was fresh snap beans from the garden and creamy baby carrots, and there was yellow cream for the apple pies, and I gave a deep sigh. Reckon we'd starve to death come winter for eating this way now, but from the drooly way I felt, I didn't much care.

Mr. Kelly stepped in the kitchen with a suitcase in his hand and his eyes popped 'most as much as mine. Almost before he could put his stuff away and come back, Clem Watts was knocking on the door. I couldn't believe my ears at the pure sweetness in Aunt Veela's voice when she said, "Why, Clem Watts, why didn't y'all let us know ye were back?" And Aunt Faith was just as sickly as she echoed Aunt Veela's welcome. Mr. Kelly and Clem said their howdys and we sat down to eat.

Clem kept staring from Aunt Veela to Aunt Faith like he couldn't believe his eyes. Mr. Kelly started bragging on the womenfolks and Aunt Hope's cooking like he usually did, and Clem tried to act nice, and the aunts preened, for all the world like hens trying to get the rooster all to themselves.

I figured grown-up folks, men and women both, were sorta addled when it come to each other, and I dug in the food fast, 'cause the way Mr. Kelly and Clem was eating, I didn't reckon on it lasting long. One thing wasn't hard to figure out, and that was the fact that Mr. Kelly and Clem

Watts didn't like each other atall. I mean, though they was real friendly with the womenfolks, they was cold polite to each other. I'd seen strange dogs that was friendlier.

The supper was so good that even when my belly screamed it was full, my mouth wanted to keep on eating. And even before the apple pie and cream came around, my belly won and all I could do was hope that there'd be some left for tomorrow.

We sat at the table so long that it was dark by the time we went to sit on the porch. Nobody but me even seemed to notice the heat.

The big summer moon was still riding low, still hot and orange-looking. We men sat on the porch, our feet on the ground, and the womenfolks took the rockers, as usual. And for the first time since I could remember, Aunt Veela didn't smoke her pipe. Nobody paid any mind to me, and the plain fact was I was the fullest and tiredest I'd ever been in my life.

The grave of Hound Dog Bates was just a shadow in the moonlight. Nobody but me even looked at it that I could tell.

Mr. Kelly and Clem (I didn't have to call him

"Mr." to myself) told big tales about cities and such, making the women laugh. Only Mr. Kelly's tales sounded like the truth and Clem's didn't. Then Clem said, "I heerd Mandy Jackson's gonna have a ba—"

"Shush yer mouth." Aunt Veela broke in sharply. "The boy's got ears, y' know."

What in the cat hair did she expect me to have? Doorknobs? I thought to myself, then stared as unconcernedly as I could across the yard so they'd think I wasn't listening. Though truth to tell, I didn't much care iffen Mandy Jackson had a dozen younguns. She already had five, and I didn't see what was special about her having another, 'less it was 'cause her husband had been in the state pen for hog stealing the last couple of years and wouldn't be home to see the new youngun for a couple more. But even that didn't matter a frog hair, 'cause I didn't have no pa looking after me and I was doing all right, or had till somebody decided to be a killer.

Tree frogs croaked with dry harsh voices, and the deep bass tones of bullfrogs on the pond joined them. Here and there was a gleam of fox fire through the trees, and a night owl hooted far off.

My eyelids slipped over my eyes like glue, and I felt myself caught before I hit the ground and faintly heard Aunt Veela saying, "Swan t' goodness. The youngun's asleep on his feet."

"Was nearly on his face." Mr. Kelly laughed, and I felt myself picked up and carried. I was shucked out of my britches like an ear of corn and lay on my bed and dreamed of chickens full of onions chasing me. Then I was trying to swim, but I couldn't 'cause the creek wasn't water but thick yellow cream. Someone put a gentle hand on me and I dreamed no more.

When I woke up at my usual time, Mr. Kelly was already missing from his bed. I could hear him talking to Aunt Hope in the kitchen. But when I got to the door they weren't talking, they was kissing! A pit opened up in my body where my belly ought to have been. A deep sadness and anger filled me. All 'cause of some danged buttermilk biscuits, Mr. Kelly had gone back on me. And I decided then and there that he liked good cooking better than me and better than finding out who killed Hound Dog Bates. And all the hurt and suspicion of the aunts came back to fill me tenfold, and my insides settled cold. And though I really had my doubts about their killing me, I knew for sure and certain they'd killed Hound Dog Bates, and I eased back where the kissing people couldn't see me and then out the door.

The rising sun cast a glow on the grave, and I told myself that the tears, every one of them, was for Hound Dog Bates, and not a one, not even the very least one, was for a big loud man who kissed dog-murdering aunts.

CHAPTER 8

"*Ye still hurtin' over yer dog, boy?*" Mr. Kelly's voice came from just behind me, and I jumped around.

I said, hissing like a snake, "Ye jest hush an' mind yer own beeswax." I felt my face go red with hate. "Yer jest a lyin', kissin' man. Ye don't nor never did keer who killed Hound Dog Bates. An' ye ain't my friend neither. Yer a woman's man"— I sneered—"jest a sissy woman's man. Ye were supposed to be my friend. I found ye first."

My voice choked off and I ran for the woods, not wanting him to see me bawling like a bull calf. 'Sides, I felt all strange. I mean, I felt all happy having Mr. Kelly for a friend, the first man friend I'd ever had, and I hated Aunt Hope and the other aunts double 'cause I figured they'd not only killed my dog but stole my friend, too.

I threw myself down under a sweet gum tree and thought Clem Watts would make a better friend than Mr. Kelly. Leastways a body could tell he was no good just by looking and listening. I buried my nose in the old rotten leaves and howled for me, Mr. Kelly, and Hound Dog Bates. When I'd cried myself out, I got up and stumbled wearily to the creek, shucked my overalls, and dove into the clean water to swim listlessly up and down till my body leastways felt clean.

I crawled out of the water and lay on the cool moss, feeling that my whole world was lonesome dark. Then something about the stillness of the woods soaked in my head, and I flew straight up, staring, feeling like a fool 'cause the world was dark, the sky a rolling twisting mass of black-purple clouds. The woods were still as death. No birds sang. Not a cricket chirped. Not one blade of grass stirred. Then far, far off I heard it, the low drone of a twister.

I looked wildly around but couldn't see which way it was coming for the thick woods, and I knowed it was only a little time till it hit. I jumped in my britches, and for somebody that had felt like dying, I was desperately looking for a place to hide so I could live.

Thunder burst the earth with sound, and lightning split the sky, turning the world a yellowish green. The tips of the tallest trees were beginning to bend. I was getting ready just to sit down and be blown to bits or smashed flat by falling trees when two big hands grabbed me and Mr. Kelly tossed me across his shoulder like I was a sack of 'taters. And he ran. He ran fast like I was nothing at all to carry. And all I could see was his heels raising up and hitting the ground, and I figured if the storm didn't get me the bouncing would. I mean, my head felt like it was going to bounce right off my neck. Probably roll under a bush and nobody'd ever find it, I thought darkly, for years and years. It'd just lay there grinning at everything that came by.

Thinking that sorta scared me, so I tried to

think of something else, like why the cow manure didn't Mr. Kelly put me down and let me run myself. Reckon he didn't know, scared as I was of storms, I could run faster than him. Fact of the matter, when I was scared enough, I could nigh fly, and with every hair I owned standing straight up on me, I knowed that I was that scared now.

I pounded on his back, but he didn't pay any more mind than if I was a black gnat buzzing around his face. The drone of the wind had turned to a low mad whine like thousands of yellow jackets in a swarm. I could feel a buzzing starting in my head, and a little in back of us I could see another man's running feet. I tried to raise my head to see who was bearing down on us. Mr. Kelly hit a pile of gravel, and my head bounced up high enough to get a glimpse of Clem Watts. Then I realized how his pa used to come to our cellar during bad weather since they didn't own one. I felt like I could dig one right here in the woods in no time flat with my bare hands if Mr. Kelly would put me down.

As if he knew what I was thinking, his arm tightened across my rear and he ran on. Clem's feet passed us and I tried to figure why Mr. Kelly would want to save me from a twister when he knowed I now hated him. Then I gave up trying to think at all 'cause I felt and heard the wind change to a loud howl, and it nigh shoved us end over end.

Mr. Kelly staggered, nigh dropping me on my head, and I let out a screech nobody could hear over the noise of the wind and bending trees, not even me.

Mr. Kelly got his bearings and ran on, but now that the wind was blowing him hither and yon and whamming my head against his broad back like a bouncing ball, I didn't know if it was the wind or my head spinning. My body sorta went out of gear when what seemed like after a week and three days Mr. Kelly came to a stop—nigh throwing me down the cellar steps for my aunts' outstretched arms to pull me down.

The heavy wooden door of the cellar slammed, and Mr. Kelly came staggering after me. It was crowded in the small storm cellar, and everybody looked pale in the coal oil lamplight. Rows and rows of canned fruit and vegetables lined the shelves. Clem Watts sat on top of the potato bin looking sick. Mr. Kelly sat on the cellar steps looking cool, calm, and cheerful like he was just taking his ease, not like he'd run with a load on his back atall.

The aunts were sitting on a bench in a row, looking like hens come to roost. Then suddenly something whammed on the cellar door like it was hit by a freight train, and the world became all noise, pounding, tearing, crashing noise that beat the earth and made it tremble. And for the first time since I was real little, since I was a baby, I went to Aunt Veela. She looked up at me, her face white and set. Then she smiled and held out her arms. And truth to tell, I crawled in them and lay my head on her shoulder and her arms felt so soft I figured right then if she was the one who killed Hound Dog Bates, then surely he must have deserved it.

Aunt Veela's overalls smelled like sun-warmed earth, ol' Sauce the mule, and corncob pipe. And underneath it all was the strange good smell of warm body and some sweet-smelling stuff like flowers. Though the aunts might go sorta out of their heads and kill a dog, I really knew they'd never hurt me on purpose. And right then and there, with the earth shaking, all fenced in warm with Aunt Veela's arms, I thought long and hard about Hound Dog Bates.

I know a body wasn't supposed to think ill of the dead, but I thought ill of him anyway. I mean, to be fair to my aunts, I had to think about Hound Dog Bates's faults as well as his good points. And truth to tell, his faults did sorta outnumber his good points. I remembered how, when he was a puppy, he peed outside till he'd see Aunt Hope looking, then he'd raise his leg and pee on anything in sight. And he did seem to have a habit of sneaking into Aunt Faith's garden to bury his bones when there was forty acres of unused ground around where he could have buried ten cows and big horses iffen he'd wanted. And truth to tell, he had a bad way of getting on Aunt Veela's nerves, too. I mean, no matter how smart and lively he'd been, when Aunt Veela came around he'd suddenly go stupid and dumb-looking, like he'd been born without one brain at all. Plumb useless was what he looked, and I couldn't fairly blame Aunt Veela for thinking that's what he was. Matter of fact, Hound Dog Bates was just flat no good for anything but me a-loving him. And I did believe he loved me too, 'cause when we was playing and he bit me too hard, he didn't never mean it. And when he slept with me and hogged the covers it was just 'cause he was colder than me. I mean he was cold-blooded. And a dog could like raw eggs. He always ate all he stole from the nests.

I knew egg money was all the money we had, but maybe Hound Dog Bates was addicted to raw eggs like some folks, Aunt Veela included, was addicted to tobacco. One thing for dang sure, Hound Dog Bates followed me around real close like a true loyal dog ought to follow a body. And if him staying too close sorta made my nerves jumpy at times, it was my fault, not his, 'cause he was just doing what a faithful dog should.

He was a joking dog, too. I mean, he loved to let a body get to sleeping good, then put his mouth in a body's ear and howl real loud. I mean, him being a dog and not being able to talk, that was the only way he had of being able to pull a trick on a person.

Thinking about it, I could sorta see somebody killing him in a fit of madness when he nigh drove them crazy. But I could see no excuse for giving ground glass, and in my heart I knew it couldn't be my aunts. But there was nobody else who knew Hound Dog Bates. And I decided if they did do it, it was because Hound Dog Bates had drove them out of their minds. And though he was my dog and I loved him, there was times when he made me forget that I did. Like the time he killed a rattlesnake and put it in my bed when I was asleep. When I woke up and seen that snake laying on the pillow next to me, I nigh died deader than the snake. 'Course Hound Dog Bates didn't know that I wouldn't know it was dead.

It was true that Hound Dog Bates came close to scaring me to death and made me pee my britches more than once, but it was also true that he kept me company on long lonely days when I was pure lonesome from a-wanting somebody of my own 'cause my aunts had to work long and hard. And I owed him something for being with me. I mean, I owed it to him to find his killer, but I also knowed that if it was one of my aunts, I didn't want to know.

I stirred in Aunt Veela's arms and realized the noise had slowed to a pounding rain. I could hear it beating against the cellar door and see little streams of water running down the cellar steps.

Still no one spoke, and it was like a deep tiredness settled over us, and there seemed nothing important enough to break the peaceful sound of rain, for it was like we were in a place where nothing mattered. Not even who killed Hound Dog Bates.

CHAPTER 9

It was Mr. Kelly who moved first. He stood up and said, "Well, let's go see if our world is still standing," and we filed silently up and out behind him. The sky was a dark gray, and rain fell in streams, but we didn't mind—for our house still stood, as did the barn. The path of the twister was no more than fifty yards away, and it had left a wide swath of twisted broken trees, some pulled up by their very roots.

Mr. Kelly mumbled, "Thank you," to saints, and

the aunts were saying, "Praise God." Clem Watts wasn't saying nothing, but he was looking mighty thankful. A lot of shingles had blown off the roof, and there were windows broken, and the cross of Hound Dog Bates's grave was blown clean away. But all in all, it was good to be cool and wet and clean-feeling.

It was nigh evening, and I felt like my belly was so empty it hung to my backbone. I still wasn't happy with Mr. Kelly for going back on me, but I wasn't going to act like it till Aunt Hope fed us. And when the food was ready, I dug into the fried potatoes and eggs nigh as hard as Mr. Kelly.

After we ate, he said, "Well, folks, we sure have our work cut out."

"And thankful we are, too, to have your help, Mr. Kelly." Aunt Hope smiled at him.

Mr. Kelly threw back his head and roared, "Well, it's the least a husband and a brother-in-law can do. And uncle—if you will have me, boy," he said, bending an eye on me.

"Ye ain't gonna be my uncle," I said, glaring at him. Then I added, "I don't like turncoats."

"Boy," he said gently, "the storm has cleared the air, an' I reckon it's time you an' me got a clear understandin' of each other. Come outside an' we'll talk."

I shook my head stubbornly, saying, "I don't wont t' talk with ye."

"We'll talk," Mr. Kelly said, and a big hand came out and lifted me off my feet and carried me like a sack of grain to the porch and out in the yard to Hound Dog Bates's grave.

Squatting so he could look me straight in the eye, Mr. Kelly said, "Now listen heer, boy, I ain't went back on ye. Didn't I tell ye I was lookin' fer a wife the day we met?"

I grudgingly nodded.

"Well, I was tellin' the truth. An' I also told ye the truth about findin' the killer of yer dog. When I went t' town t' git my things, I asked the store owner who'd bought poison from his store. An' it was Clem Watts. He'd bought poison for weasels that was killin' his chickens an' stealin' his eggs. An' the rest of the detective work is easy. Yer dog was found near the Watts place, which meant he had been there. He had been where he wasn't s'posed t' be. Now, boy, I'll tell ye somethin' else. I don't believe in poisonin' animals of any sort, an' reckon Clem Watts won't either when I git through with him," and looking at him, I knew he was telling the truth.

All of a sudden I felt a loving in me for this huge kind man, and I was sure glad he was to be my uncle. I didn't know how to tell him, but reckon he knowed, for we just grinned at each other for a while. Then he said, "Well, boy, I have t' see a man about a dog," and he went off down the same road that Clem Watts had taken not long before.

I sat by my dog's grave and thought it had to be a pure fact that it was Hound Dog Bates stealing Clem Watts' eggs. And truth to tell, I'd felt for a long time Hound Dog Bates would have been a chicken killer iffen he could have got away with it. I mean, the way he eyed our chickens at times. And reckon that the dog was the weasel Clem Watts was trying to kill, and it was poison bait that killed him, not ground glass atall.

Ye shore ain't much punkins as a detective, I told myself bitterly. Then thinking of Mr. Kelly, I felt better. I mean, I bet me and him could have us a dozen dogs and the aunts wouldn't say a word to him.

I got up from beside the grave in the dripping

rain and went to find nails and boards to nail another cross together. I heard the aunts calling back and forth to each other cheerfully, and I was thinking maybe they was more hopeful having Mr. Kelly to take some of the workload off their shoulders and reckoned I was man enough to do more, too. I bet, with Mr. Kelly in our family, we'd go to church and Aunt Veela would wear dresses on Sunday and Aunt Faith would keep wearing ribbons and Aunt Hope would bake every day.

The rain made my pocketknife slick, and it took me a long time to finish the carving. When we sat on the porch that evening, the setting sun drying up the wetness, all of them could plainly see the carving on the cross, and they knew I no longer felt suspicion or distrust of the three aunts who had given up a life of their own to raise me, for on the cross I had carved, "Here lies Hound Dog Bates who committed suicide by his own mouth fer a-eatin' thing or things unknown t' be pizen. This truth wuz found out by his master Sassafras Bates and his uncle Mister Kelly O'Kelly."